Halloween with Morris and Boris

Written and illustrated by BERNARD WISEMAN

SCHOLASTIC BOOK SERVICES

NEW YORK · TORONTO · LONDON · AUCKLAND · SYDNEY · TOKYO

For Susan, Peter, and Willi

ISBN: 0-590-01530-3

Copyright © 1975 by Bernard Wiseman. This edition is published by Scholastic Book Services, a division of Scholastic Magazines, Inc., by arrangement with Dodd, Mead and Company.

13 12 11 10 9 8 7 6

1 2 3 4 5 6/8
07

Boris the Bear yelled,
"Hooray! Halloween is here."

Morris the Moose said,
"Halloween is not here.
I don't see him."

Boris said,
"Halloween is not a him.
Halloween is a…"

"I know!" cried Morris.
"Halloween is a her."

"No!" Boris said.
"Halloween is a holiday.
It is when
children make pumpkins..."

Morris laughed.
"Children can't make pumpkins.
Pumpkins grow."

"I know that!" Boris shouted.
"Let me finish. It is when children
make pumpkins into Jack-o'-Lanterns."

"Into what?" asked Morris.

"Oh, come with me," Boris said.
"I will show you."

"There," said Boris, "you see?
Children make eyes and mouths
in pumpkins. Then the pumpkins
are Jack-o'-Lanterns."

Morris said, "I would make
a Morris-o'-Lantern."

Boris yelled,
"They are always called
Jack-o'-Lanterns!"

"Jack is a boy's name," said Morris.
"Don't girls make Jill-o'-Lanterns?"

"No!" shouted Boris.

Morris said, "Oh—Halloween is
just for boys. Not for girls."

"NO! NO!" Boris roared. "Halloween
is for girls, too. I will show you."

Boris said, "Look—
one of those children
is a girl."

"They are not children!" cried Morris.
"One is made of bones!
One has a pointed head! Eeeoww!
I am scared. I am going home."

Boris laughed.
"They are just children.
They are dressed up
to play Trick-or-Treat.
They ring doorbells
or knock on doors.
They say Trick-or-Treat,
and people give them candy."

Morris asked, "Did you say CANDY?"

Boris said, "Yes, I said candy."

Morris said,
"Then you mean Trick-or-EAT!
Let's play it. I want candy."

Boris said,
"It is called Trick-or-Treat.
We can't play it.
We have no costumes."

"No what?" Morris asked.

"Costumes," Boris told him.
"What the children are wearing."

Morris said, "I can make
your head pointed..."

Boris roared, "ROWRRR!"
And he chased Morris.

They ran into a backyard.
Morris ran past a clothesline—

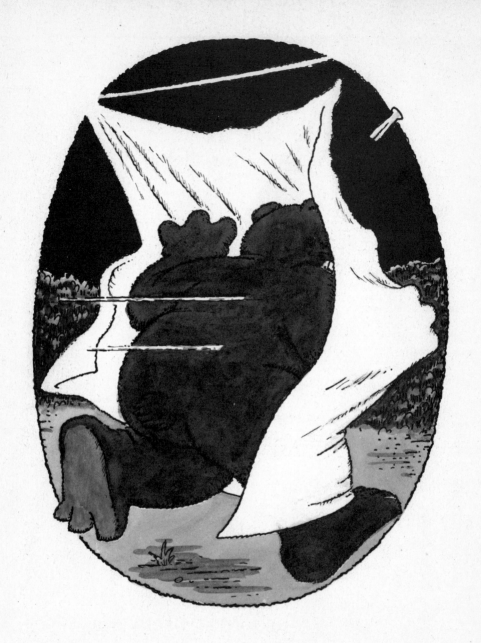

Boris ran into the clothesline.

"Look!" Boris cried. "I have
a costume. I am a ghost."

"A what?" Morris asked.

"A ghost," Boris said.
"Something that makes you scared."

Morris laughed.
"You are not a ghost.
You do not scare me."

Boris yelled, "BOO!"

Morris yelled, "YEEEOWWW!
You ARE a ghost!"
And Morris started to run again.

He ran into a garage.
BANG! CLANG! BONG!

He ran out of the garage...

...into some garbage cans.
CLANG! CLUNG! BOONG!

"Look!" said Boris.
"Now YOU have a costume.
You are a clown."

"A what?" asked Morris.

"A clown," Boris said.
"Someone who makes you laugh."

Morris said, "I am a clown.
Now we can play Trick-or-Treat
and get candy."

Morris went to one house.
He did not get candy.

Morris went to another house.
He still did not get candy.

"Oh, let me do it!" Boris cried.
And he rang a doorbell.

A lady opened the door.
When she saw Boris
she yelled, "YEEEOWWW!"

Boris did not get candy.
"Let me do it," Morris said.
And he rang the doorbell.

The lady opened the door again.
When she saw Morris she laughed.
Morris said, "Trick-or-Treat."
The lady gave him candy.

Morris rang another doorbell.
A man opened the door.

Morris's mouth was full of candy.
He could not say Trick-or-Treat.
He said, "Twick-or-Tweet."
The man laughed
and gave Morris more candy.

Boris cried, "I want to get candy!
Let's change costumes."

Morris and Boris changed costumes...

...and Boris got candy.

At the next house a girl opened the door.

"Come in!" she cried. "We are having
a Halloween party."

Morris and Boris
went into the house.

They saw apples
in a big bowl of water.
Children were trying
to pick up the apples
with their teeth.

Morris said, "Oh, they do not want
to wet their hands."
And Morris gave apples to
the children.

"No!" Boris cried. "This is a game.
It is called Bobbing-for-Apples.
You must pick up the apples
with your teeth."

Morris liked apples.
He picked up
all the apples with his teeth.
Boris yelled, "You did not
leave any for me!"

"Yes I did," said Morris.

The girl said, "Let's play
Pin-the-Tail-on-the-Donkey."

She hung up
a picture of a donkey.
With their eyes covered,
they all tried
to pin a tail on the donkey.

This time Boris made a mistake.

Then they ate cake and ice cream.

Morris did not sit down to eat.

And then a boy said,
"Let's turn off the lights
and tell ghost stories."

"Let's tell what?" Morris asked.

"Ghost stories," the boy said.
"Stories that scare you."

Morris laughed.
"Ghost stories will not scare me."

They turned off the lights
and told ghost stories.

Morris did not get scared.

But then Morris went to
the bathroom.

There was a mirror in there.
Morris yelled,
"YEEEOWWW! A GHOST!"

And Morris began to run again.

"Wait!" Boris shouted.
"Halloween is over.
We must put back our costumes."

Morris and Boris put back
the costumes. Morris said,
"Now I will not
get scared anymore."

Just then Boris put the covers
back on the garbage cans.
CLANG! CLUNG! CLANGGG!

Morris yelled, "YEEEOWWW!"
And he began to run again.
Boris ran after him,
all the way home.